On Market Street

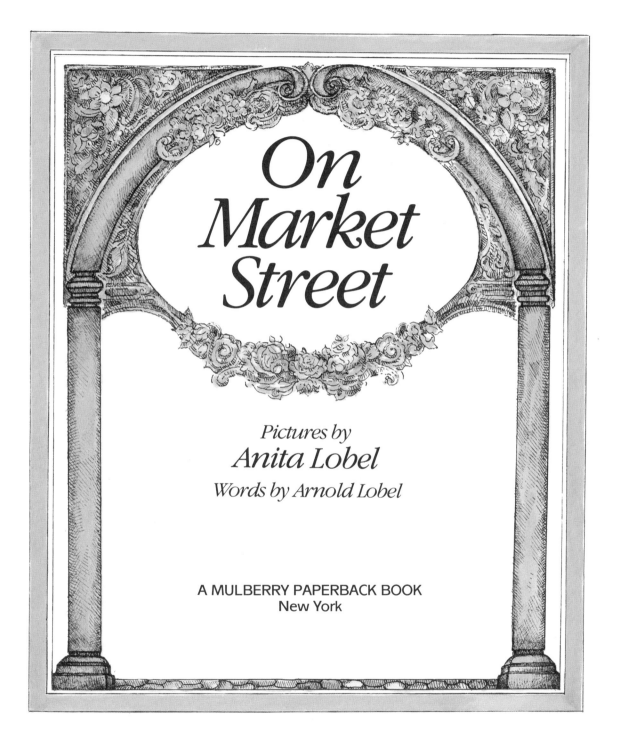

On Market Street

Pictures by
Anita Lobel
Words by Arnold Lobel

A MULBERRY PAPERBACK BOOK
New York

Printed in the United States of America   First Mulberry Edition, 1989   10 9 8 7 6 5

Library of Congress Cataloging in Publication Data   Lobel, Arnold.   On Market Street.
Summary: A child buys presents from A to Z in the shops along Market Street.
[1. Shopping—Fiction. 2. Alphabet. 3. Stories in rhyme] I. Lobel, Anita. II. Title.
PZ8.3.L820m [E]   80-21418   ISBN 0-688-08745-0

To Timothy and Susan Benn

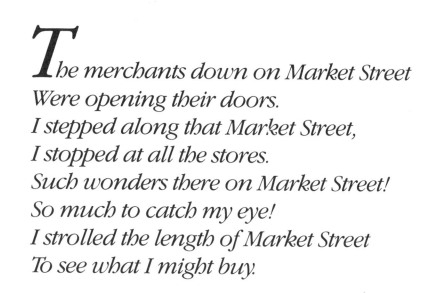

The merchants down on Market Street
Were opening their doors.
I stepped along that Market Street,
I stopped at all the stores.
Such wonders there on Market Street!
So much to catch my eye!
I strolled the length of Market Street
To see what I might buy.

And I bought…

apples,

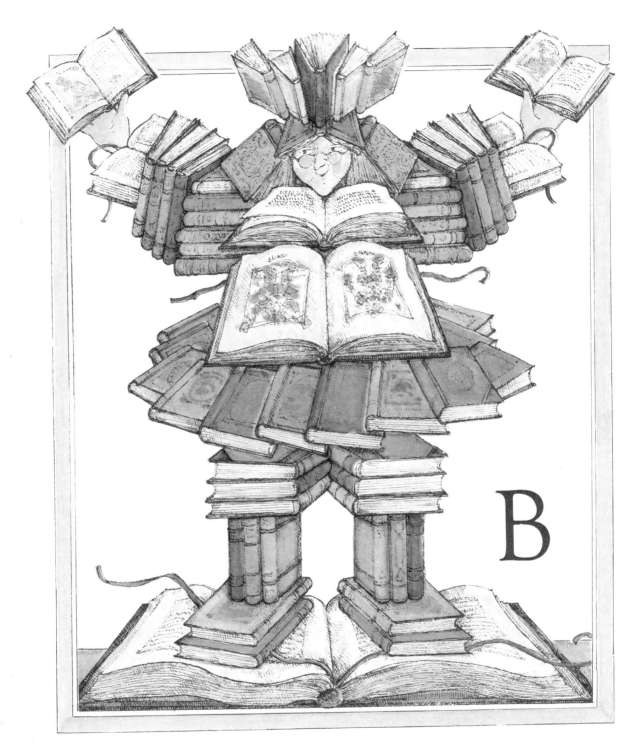

B

books,

clocks,

doughnuts,

eggs,

flowers,

gloves,

hats,

ice cream,

jewels,

K

kites,

lollipops,

M

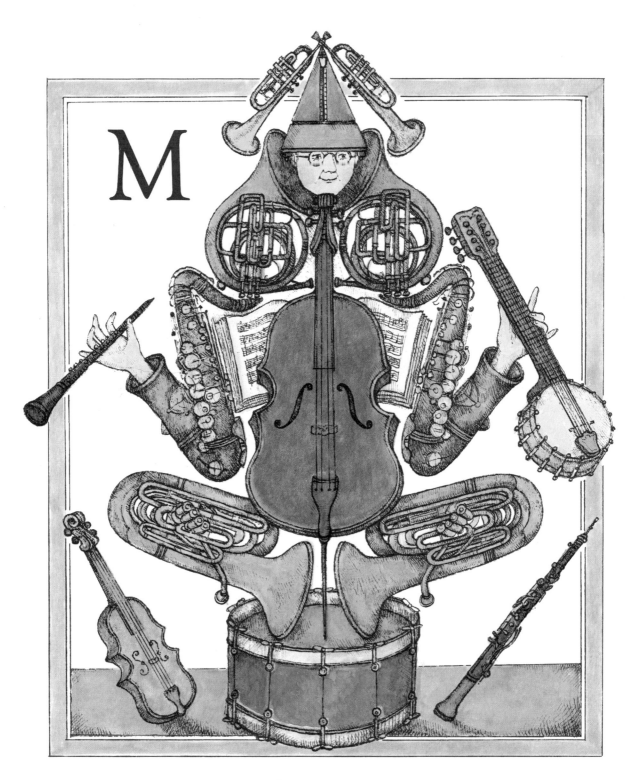

musical instruments,

noodles,

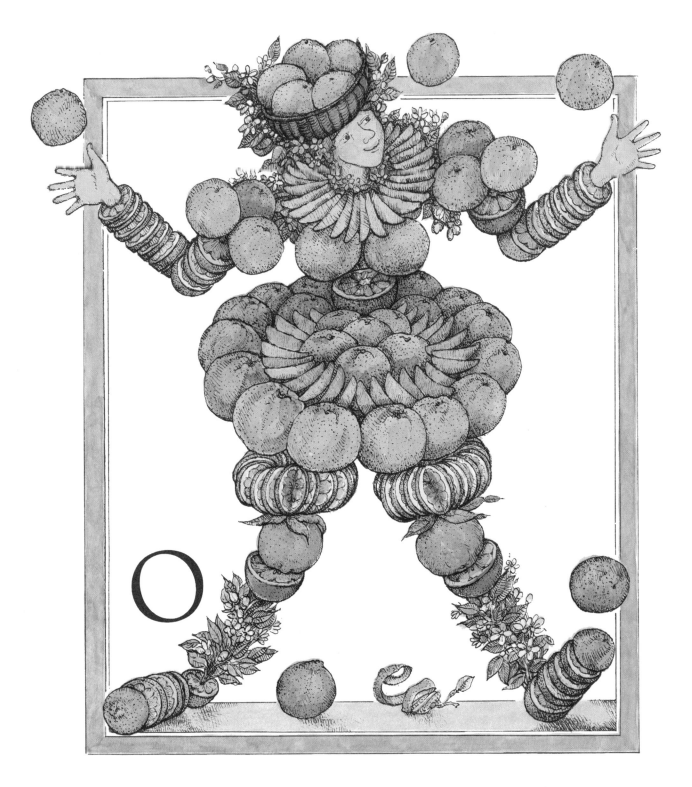

O

oranges,

P

playing cards,

quilts,

ribbons,

S

shoes,

toys,

U

umbrellas,

V

vegetables,

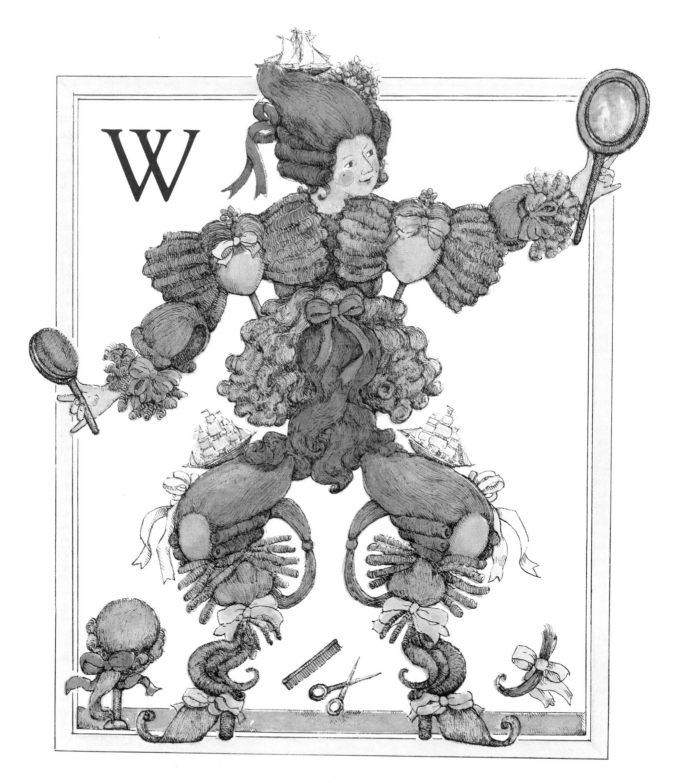

wigs,

Xmas trees,

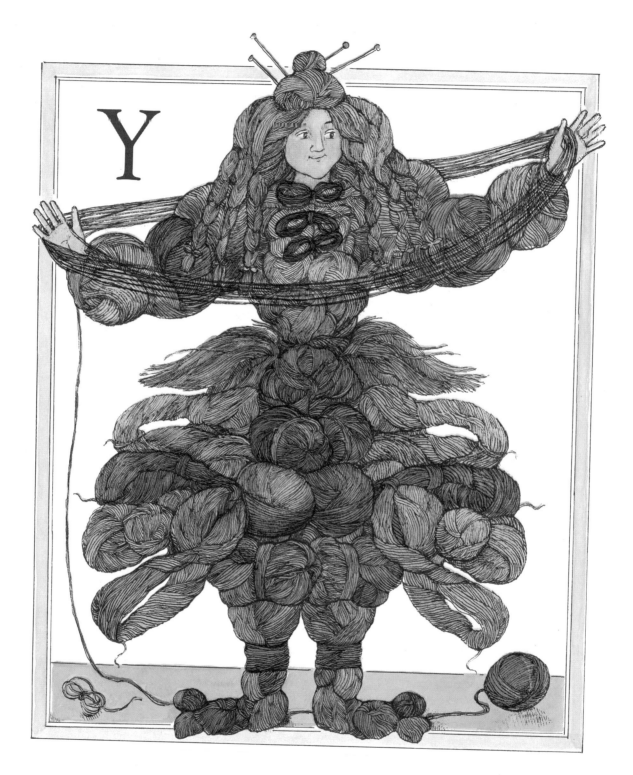

yarns,

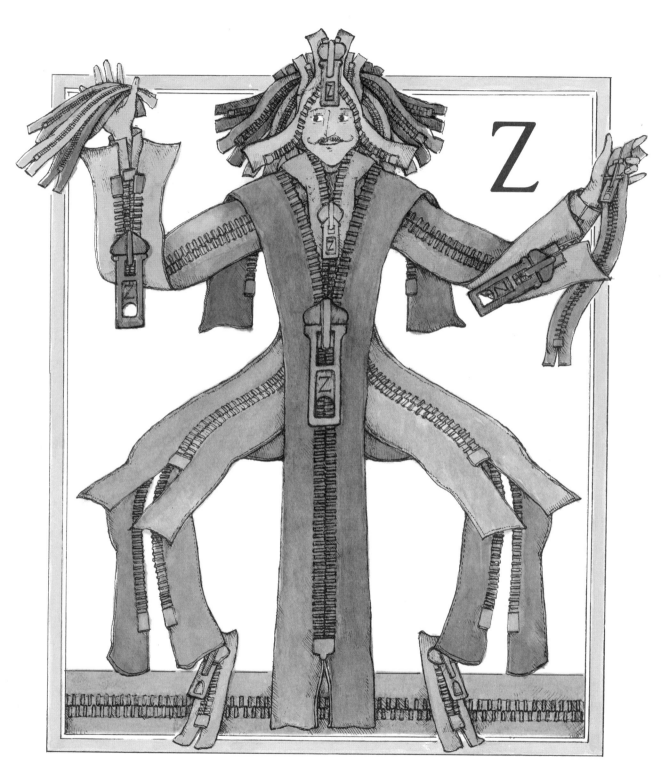

zippers.

My arms were full on Market Street,
I could not carry more.
As darkness fell on Market Street,
My feet were tired and sore.
But I was glad on Market Street,
These coins I brought to spend,
I spent them all on Market Street…

...on presents for a friend.

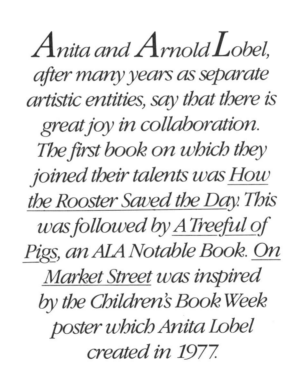

Anita and Arnold Lobel, after many years as separate artistic entities, say that there is great joy in collaboration. The first book on which they joined their talents was <u>How the Rooster Saved the Day</u>. This was followed by <u>A Treeful of Pigs</u>, an ALA Notable Book. <u>On Market Street</u> was inspired by the Children's Book Week poster which Anita Lobel created in 1977.